Rugrats

Chuckie's New Mommy

adapted by Kim Ostrow
based on a screenplay by Sarah Cunningham and Suzie Villandry
illustrated by Robert Roper

SIMON SPOTLIGHT
An imprint of Simon & Schuster Children's Publishing Division
New York   London   Toronto   Sydney   Singapore
1230 Avenue of the Americas, New York, New York 10020
Copyright © 2002 Viacom International Inc. All rights reserved.
NICKELODEON, *Rugrats*, and all related titles, logos, and characters are trademarks of Viacom International Inc.
All rights reserved, including the right of reproduction in whole or in part in any form.
SIMON SPOTLIGHT and colophon are registered trademarks of Simon & Schuster.
Manufactured in the United States of America   ISBN 0-689-84606-1 First Edition
2 4 6 8 10 9 7 5 3 1

KLASKY
CSUPO INC.

Based on the TV series *Rugrats*® created by Arlene Klasky, Gabor Csupo, and Paul Germain as seen on Nickelodeon®

"Here I am!" shouted Chuckie as he burst through the bushes.

"Chuckie, you're opposed to wait until I finded you," said Tommy.

"Oh, yeah," said Chuckie. "I forgotted again."

Kimi popped out from behind another bush. "Here I am!" she cried happily.

"Uh . . . let's play something else," Chuckie mumbled.

As the babies headed for the sandbox Chuckie stopped short.

"Oh, no, here she comes," said Chuckie. "My new mommy's gonna do it again."

"Do what?" asked Tommy.

"She's gonna smoosh down my hairs," Chuckie said nervously. "I just know it."

"Hi, Kimi. Hi, Chuckie," Kira said. "Ready to go home?"

Chuckie tried to duck out of the way as Kira came closer, but it was too late.

"Is everything okay with Chuckie?" Didi asked Kira.

"I don't know," answered Kira. "I feel like we're not connecting. And with Chas working late these days, I worry that Chuckie may feel unsettled."

"Maybe Dr. Lipschitz can help," said Didi. "I'll call the 800 number and ask if they can recommend a book about new families."

Kira nodded. "That's exactly what I need."

Back at home Chuckie sat in his new big-boy chair and stared at the mountain of food in front of him.

"Kimi, what is this stuff?" he asked. "It looks like squiggly worms with mud balls on top."

"It's pasghetti and meatyballs!" said Kimi. "My mommy makes it all the time. It's her specialty."

"I never eated nuthin' like that afore," Chuckie grumbled.

Chuckie piled a meatball onto his fork and tried to eat it. But it wouldn't fit in his mouth.

"AH-CHOO!" Chuckie sneezed, and the meatball fell to the floor. "These meatyballs are so big, the sauce gets in my nose and gives me the sneezies," said Chuckie unhappily.

"They don't give me the sneezies," said Kimi. "And I eats them all the time."

Kira gently wiggled a tissue over Chuckie's nose. Chuckie squirmed in his seat.

"How am I opposed to blow my nose on a wigglin' tissue, Kimi?" asked Chuckie when Kira was gone.

"Mommy always holds my tissue," said Kimi. "I like it."

"Well, I don't," mumbled Chuckie. So he blew his nose the way he liked—on his sleeve.

After dinner Chuckie and Kimi got ready for b

"I don't like these new jammies," Chuckie said

"My feets are trapped and I can't wiggle my toes.

"But they keep your toesies warm," said Kimi.

"My jammies gots feets, my meatyballs are sneezy, my hairs are smooshy," complained Chuckie. "Nothing's the same."

Just then Kira came in to say good night. "Sweet dreams," she said as she turned off the light.

"Looks like you needs a hug, Wawa," said Chuckie, clutching his teddy bear. "At least we gots each other. And that's never, ever gonna change."

Later that night Didi dropped off a present for Kira. It was Dr. Lipschitz's bestselling book, *Step Up to Stepparenting*.

"'Chapter One,'" Kira read out loud, "'Connecting with Your Stepchild.'" She thumbed through the pages until she found a suggestion that sounded just right.

Kira headed upstairs to check on Chuckie and Kimi. As she smoothed Chuckie's hair Kira noticed his tattered teddy bear.

"Looks like somebody needs a makeover," she said to herself as she scooped up Wawa. "Chuckie will be so surprised!"

"Meatyballs . . . jammy feets . . . smooshy hairs . . . ,"
Chuckie moaned, tossing and turning in his bed. Then he felt
around for his Wawa. Chuckie's eyes popped open. "Wawa's
gone!"

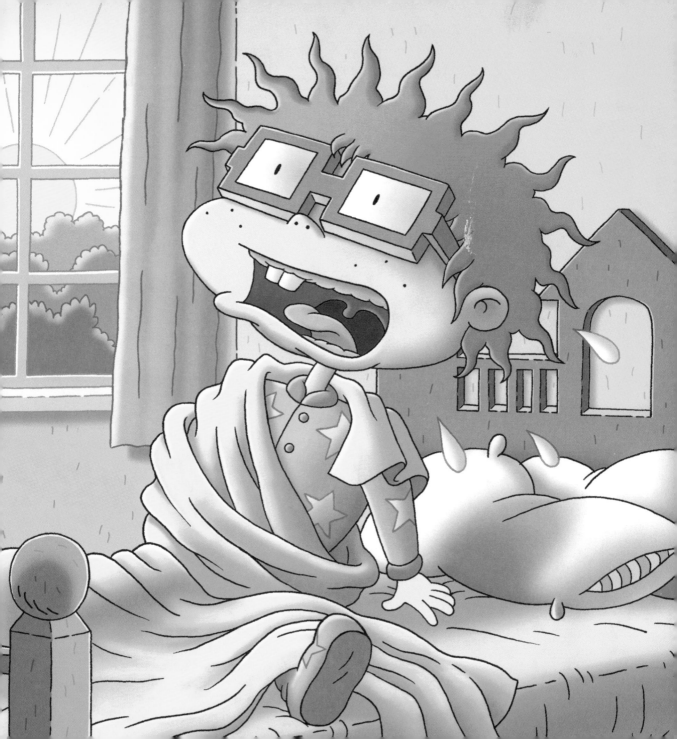

At breakfast Chuckie slumped in his chair.

"What's wrong, Chuckie?" whispered Tommy.

"Nothin' is the same now that I gots a new mommy," Chuckie said sadly. "So Wawa runned away."

"When I gots Dilly, lotsa stuffs changed for me too," said Tommy. "But now everything's all better."

SPLAT! Dil threw a glob of cereal that landed on Tommy's head.

"I dunno, Tommy," said Chuckie. "Wawa's gone and he's never coming back."

"Sure he is, Chuckie!" assured Tommy. "We'll help you find him."

The babies toddled down the hall to look for the missing teddy bear.
"Maybe Wawa's in the lawn-tree room," Kimi suggested.
"He's not under here," said Tommy.
"Not in here, either," said Kimi.
Chuckie thought he felt something soft and warm in the sock basket.
"Wawa!" he shouted. But it was just Fifi taking a nap. Chuckie sighed.
"I'm never gonna see my Wawa again."

"There you are," said Kira. "I have a special surprise for you, Chuckie!" She opened the dryer and pulled out a freshly washed, newly dressed, cleaned-up teddy bear.

"Aaaaaaarggh!" Chuckie screamed. He knocked Wawa out of Kira's hands and ran upstairs.

"Chuckie! What's wrong?" cried Kira as she ran after him.

Chuckie's teddy bear had landed on Dil's bouncy seat. As Didi straightened the laundry room, Dil chewed on Wawa's ear.

Then he tore off the little vest that Kira had put on Wawa.

When Dil threw the bear up in the air . . .

. . Wawa landed in a sudsy bucket, pilling it all over the floor.
Didi spun around. "Uh-oh, I hink it's time to go!"

"I guess there's still a lot I don't know about you," Kira said sweetly, "like your favorite food, or your favorite games, or the stories you like." Kira moved closer. "It may take me a little while to figure it out, so until then, I'll tell you the one thing I do know. I know I have a new little boy who I love very much."

Chuckie looked up at his new mommy and smiled. But when she tried to smooth his hair, he cringed. And Kira finally understood. Instead of smoothing Chuckie's hair, this time she messed it up. Chuckie giggled and Kira giggled too. Then they gave each other a great big hug.

"Looks like Dil got a hold of Wawa," Kira said. "He's back the way you like him." She handed Chuckie the bear.

Chuckie hugged his tattered bear and smiled. "My new mommy may not be perfect, but she's mine!"

STECK-VAUGHN
Elements of Reading

Level C

Vocabulary

Isabel L. Beck, Ph.D., and Margaret G. McKeown, Ph.D.

This book belongs to

Harcourt Achieve

Rigby • Steck-Vaughn

www.HarcourtAchieve.com
1.800.531.5015

Acknowledgments

Editorial Director Stephanie Muller

Lead Editor Terra Tarango

Editor Victoria Davis

Design Team Cynthia Ellis, Alexandra Corona, Joan Cunningham

Production Team Mychael Ferris-Pacheco, Paula Schumann, Alan Klemp

Editorial, Design, and Production Development The Quarasan Group, Inc.

Illustrations: Anthony Accardo 67; Susan Banta 15, 44; Kristin Barr 31; Amy Bishop 18; Thomas Buchs 72; Lindy Burnett 3, 50; Priscilla Burris 26, 55; Laurie Conley 40, 86; Nancy Didion iii, 23, 70; Angela Donato 14; Drew-Brook-Cormack Assoc. 8, 42; Teddy Edinjiklian 16, 34, 58, 62, 95; Doreen Gay-Kassel 20, 68; Diane Greenseid 2; Meryl Henderson 10; Richard Hoit 99; Nicole in den Bosch 98; Flora Jew 96; Diana Kizlauskas 28, 74; Barbara Lanza 24; Jeff LeVan 27, 54, 88; Brian Lies 80; Loretta Lustig 6, 36, 60, 87; Erin Mauterer 4, 7, 52, 83; Diana McFarland 35, 82; Carol Newsom 39; Ed Olson 12, 59, 90; Philomena O'Neill 30; David Opie 43, 71; Mark Page 48; Lori Pandy 66; Karen Pellaton 76; Gary Phillips 32, 92; Janice Skivington-Wood 46, 78; Bridget Starr Taylor iv, 64; Neecy Twinem 51, 75; Laura Watson 1; Siri Weber Feeney 84

ISBN 0-7398-8448-4

© 2005 Harcourt Achieve Inc.

Dear Teacher,

This Student Book is full of lively, fun-filled activities that provide ample opportunities for students to practice using new words.

The vocabulary words in this book are meant to increase students' oral vocabulary skills, so the activities are designed to be led by the teacher. Use the teacher notes at the bottom of each page in conjunction with the Word Chats in the Teacher's Guide to facilitate engaging discussions surrounding these activities.

While this book is for children, we hope that you will have fun, too! The more you use and have fun with new words, the more your students will enjoy and use them, too.

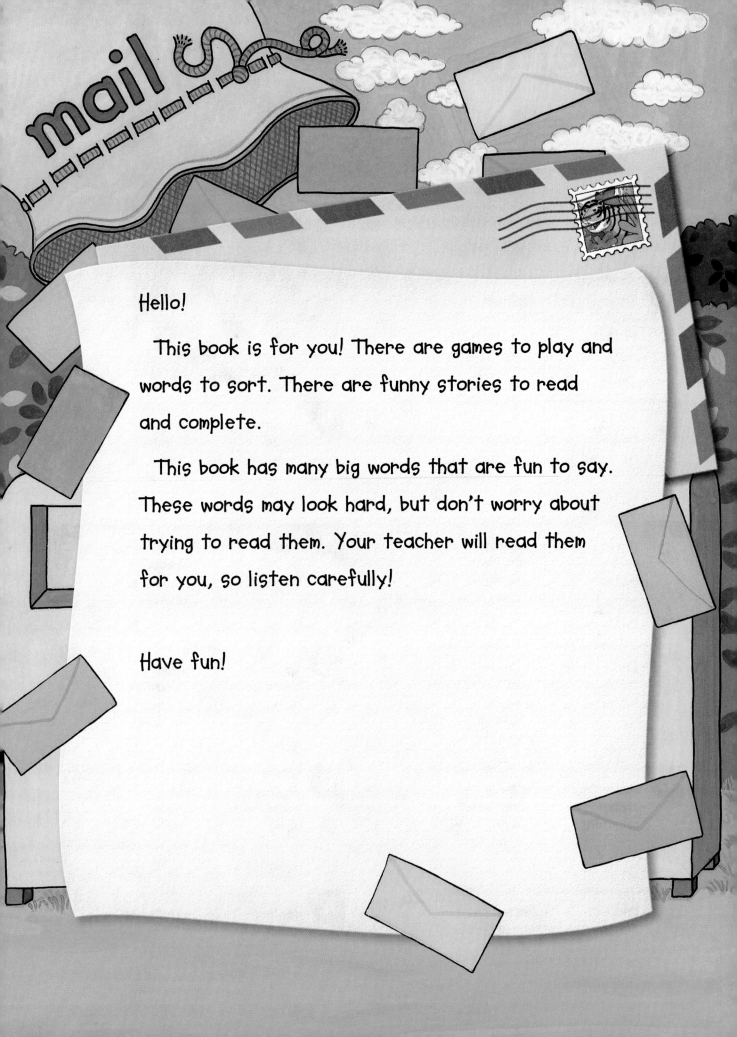

Hello!

This book is for you! There are games to play and words to sort. There are funny stories to read and complete.

This book has many big words that are fun to say. These words may look hard, but don't worry about trying to read them. Your teacher will read them for you, so listen carefully!

Have fun!

Contents

expression

shelter

comforting

fleet

vital

glimmer

versatile

1

2

3

4

Teacher: Read aloud the vocabulary words. Have students look at each picture and write the vocabulary word that best describes it. Ask students which word they wrote under each picture and why.

Listen. Read. Write.

1

A _____ Place

Versatile

Expression

Vital

"Welcome to the Treetown Home for Animals!" said the caregiver. The children were amazed at all the playful animals. Kittens and puppies were chasing balls and toy mice. A kitten leapt onto the caregiver's shoulder. "The animals here are all full of life," the caregiver explained. "We have people come in every day to play with them all!"

2

A Silly _____

Ana loved the clowns in the circus. Patches was her favorite. Although Patches didn't talk, Ana could watch his face and tell what the clown was thinking. His playful grin always made Ana laugh.

3

A _____ Boy

Julia was amazed at everything her older brother could do. He was good in math and science. He loved music and sports. Julia told her friends, "Jason can do anything and everything!"

Teacher: Read aloud the vocabulary words at the top of the page. Have students read the stories and write a vocabulary word to complete each title. Ask students which words they chose to complete the titles and why.

3

Listen. Read. Write.

twinkle

safe

swift

protect

cover

sparkle

speedy

shine

quick

fleet

glimmer

shelter

_____

_____

_____

_____

_____

_____

_____

_____

_____

4

Teacher: Read aloud the vocabulary words that appear on each cloud. Have students read the words on the stars and write each word under its related vocabulary word. Ask students which words they wrote on each cloud and why.

1 What would be **comforting** to a baby?
- ○ rumbling thunder
- ○ a quiet lullaby
- ○ a scratchy blanket

2 Where might a hiker find **shelter** from a storm?
- ○ in a field
- ○ in a school
- ○ in a cave

3 What would a **fleet** animal do?
- ○ chirp cheerfully
- ○ move quickly
- ○ snore loudly

4 Which would **glimmer** at night?
- ○ the headlights of a car
- ○ the flame of a candle
- ○ a bright streetlight

5 Where might you see a surprised **expression**?
- ○ on someone's face
- ○ in a puddle
- ○ on a daisy

6 What would a **vital** person say?
- ○ "Let's take a rest."
- ○ "Let's jog around the block."
- ○ "I'm so sorry."

7 Which piece of clothing is the most **versatile**?
- ○ a tuxedo
- ○ a bathing suit
- ○ a T-shirt

Teacher: Read aloud each numbered item and have students fill in the bubble next to the correct answer.

Listen. Write.

1 Molly was tired. She felt like stretching out on the car seat, but she knew that she wouldn't be safe. Instead she decided to sit up and **fasten** her seatbelt.

_____

_____

fasten

_____

2 Chad and Peter practice tennis together. Playing with a **companion** is more fun than playing alone.

_____

companion

3 Otto and Oscar Otter liked to **tease** Bert Beaver. Sometimes they would not let him play with them.

_____

_____

tease

Teacher: Read aloud each numbered item. Have students write the vocabulary word under the picture that shows its meaning. Ask students which picture they chose and why.

One afternoon Rick and his friends were hanging out in the park. "Here comes that new kid Sam," Kenny said. "Let's ask him to play ball with us."

"He never smiles," said Jack. "Having him around wouldn't be much fun!"

"Some kids think he's stuck up," Rick said, "but maybe he just misses his old friends. I have an idea."

When Sam walked by, Rick invited him to join the group. Before long they were chatting about their favorite sports and TV shows they liked. Suddenly Sam was smiling. He was sure he had found three new friends.

serious

assume

hopeful

lonely

companions

1 Rick and his friends are _____ who spend a lot of time together.

2 Jack thinks Sam is too _____ to be any fun.

3 Kids _____ that Sam is stuck up.

4 Rick thinks Sam might be feeling _____.

5 At the end of the story, Sam feels _____ that he has found some new friends.

Teacher: Have students read the story. Then read the vocabulary words aloud. Have students read the sentences and write the vocabulary word that best completes each sentence. Ask students which words they wrote and why.

7

Listen. Read. Write.

Walt Walrus loved playing in the snow with his pals. He _____ he would see his _____ sliding down the snowbanks, shouting and laughing. But today the hills were quiet. Walt hurried to the pond, _____ that he would find his friends, but nobody was there. Walt felt cold and _____. Walt _____ his jacket as he considered this _____ problem. Suddenly Walt looked up and saw his friends sliding toward him on a huge sled. "Jump on," they _____, as the sled flew past.

teased   lonely
serious   fastened
assumed   hopeful
companions

Teacher: Read aloud the vocabulary words at the top of the page. Then have students read the story and write the best words to fill in the blanks. Ask students which words they chose to complete the story and why.

1 How would you feel if someone **teased** you?
- ○ happy and grateful
- ○ hurt and angry
- ○ silly and tired

2 What could make someone feel **lonely**?
- ○ breaking a window
- ○ losing a best friend
- ○ being late for dinner

3 When would someone want to be **serious**?
- ○ playing catch with a friend
- ○ playing tag on the playground
- ○ playing a game of chess

4 What would be easy to **fasten** together?
- ◉ a baseball and a bat
- ◉ a ribbon and a string
- ◉ a bottle and a can

5 What would be dangerous to **assume**?
- ○ your bed is comfortable
- ○ your house is fireproof
- ○ your dinner is ready

6 What might a **hopeful** person believe?
- ○ that her party will be a big success
- ○ that no one will come to her party
- ○ that her party will be rained out

7 Who might make the best **companions**?
- ○ a dog and a child
- ○ a child and a lion
- ○ a bullfrog and a fly

Teacher: Read aloud each numbered item and have students fill in the bubble next to the correct answer.

9

tremble   boast

giddy   stranded   resourceful

consequence

rescue

_____

_____

_____

_____

Teacher: Read aloud the vocabulary words. Have
students look at each picture and write the vocabulary
word that best describes it. Ask students which word they
wrote under each picture and why.

Listen. Read. Write.

1 The cat was **stranded** in a very tall tree. It was not able to climb down because it was _____.

dirty
stuck
hungry

2 Ashley is a very **resourceful** person. She can _____ almost any problem that comes up.

create
solve
remember

3 Firefighters **rescue** people from burning buildings. They are probably some of the _____ people alive.

meanest
funniest
bravest

4 Sarah likes to **boast** whenever she gets a good grade. Her classmates think that she is too _____.

greedy
proud
shy

5 Jake had to accept the **consequence** of not saving his money. He _____ buy a new bicycle.

couldn't
wouldn't
should

Teacher: Read aloud each pair of sentences. Have students read the word choices and write the best word to fill in the blank. Ask students which words they chose and why.

11

Listen. Read. Write.

ideas

shake

angry

scared

solve

joyful

clever

shiver

happy

silly

smart

foolish

giddy	resourceful	tremble

Teacher: Read aloud the vocabulary words that appear on the shelves. Have students read the words on the cans and write each word under its related vocabulary word. Ask students which words they wrote on each shelf and why.

12

1 What might a **giddy** person do?
- ○ make funny faces
- ○ cough and sneeze
- ○ fall asleep

2 What might someone **boast** about?
- ○ breaking a dish
- ○ winning a contest
- ○ forgetting a name

3 What could cause someone to be **stranded**?
- ○ missing a day of school
- ○ missing a meal
- ○ missing a bus

4 Which of these might make you **tremble**?
- ○ a colorful painting
- ○ a strange noise
- ○ a shiny penny

5 What might you **rescue** someone from?
- ○ being outside in a snowstorm
- ○ sitting in a flower garden
- ○ taking an exciting vacation

6 Which words describe a **resourceful** person?
- ○ selfish and mean
- ○ gentle and kind
- ○ clever and creative

7 What might be a **consequence** of not getting enough sleep?
- ○ staying up too late
- ○ feeling tired
- ○ cleaning your bedroom

Teacher: Read aloud each numbered item and have students fill in the bubble next to the correct answer.

13

1 Mary needed a dress to wear to her sister's wedding. She tried on a plain dress that fit her perfectly. Then she saw a fancy dress with lace. Mary chose the **elegant** dress.

_____

elegant

_____

2 A squirrel was hiding in Bill's garage. Bill put out some acorns. He hoped the squirrel would **emerge** so he could catch it.

_____

_____

emerge

3 A man on the corner was playing music. Mark saw people drop coins into the man's jar. Mark decided to **contribute**, too.

contribute

_____

_____

Teacher: Read aloud each numbered item. Have students write the vocabulary word under the picture that shows its meaning. Ask students which picture they chose and why.

14

Every summer a special event takes place in a tiny village tucked away in the jungle. Tigers and cheetahs come out of their dens. Chimpanzees swing down from the treetops. The elephants gather flowers and set a beautiful table in the clearing. The zebras put together a fantastic feast of tasty fruits and vegetables. All the jungle creatures bring something to share. There are games and contests of all kinds. At the end of the day, everyone is tired, but they will talk about the event for weeks to come.

nestled

assemble

emerge

weary

nutritious

1 The tiny village is _____ in the jungle.

2 Tigers and cheetahs _____ from their dens.

3 The zebras _____ food for the feast.

4 The feast of tasty fruits and vegetables is _____.

5 At the end of a long day, everyone is _____.

Teacher: Have students read the story. Then read the vocabulary words aloud. Have students read the sentences and write the vocabulary word that best completes each sentence. Ask students which words they wrote and why.

Listen. Read. Write.

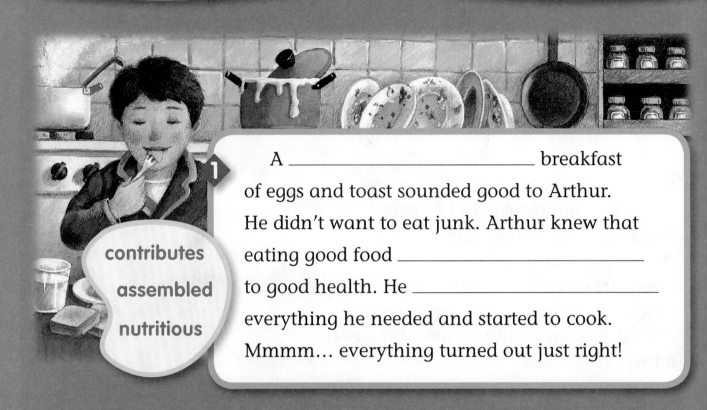

1 A _____ breakfast of eggs and toast sounded good to Arthur. He didn't want to eat junk. Arthur knew that eating good food _____ to good health. He _____ everything he needed and started to cook. Mmmm… everything turned out just right!

contributes

assembled

nutritious

2 The baby raccoon _____ sleepily against its mother. Their home in the hollow tree is not _____, but it is snug and warm. When spring comes, the creatures will _____ to romp and play. For now, however, this home is a safe place for the _____ raccoons to rest.

nestles

elegant

emerge

weary

Teacher: Read aloud the vocabulary words in the shapes. Then have students read the stories and write the best words to fill in the blanks. Ask students which words they chose to complete each story and why.

1 What might someone **nestle** in their arms?
- ○ a rock
- ○ a pencil
- ○ a teddy bear

2 What could make someone become **weary**?
- ○ picking some flowers
- ○ running a long race
- ○ relaxing on a sofa

3 What would you wear something **elegant** to?
- ○ a beach party
- ○ a baseball game
- ○ an expensive restaurant

4 What might a fox **emerge** from?
- ○ a subway in the city
- ○ a hole in the ground
- ○ a swimming pool

5 Which would be a **nutritious** snack?
- ○ a handful of nuts
- ○ a handful of chocolates
- ○ a handful of potato chips

6 Which might you need to **assemble**?
- ○ a bicycle
- ○ a butterfly
- ○ a bathtub

7 Which might someone **contribute** money to?
- ○ a gasoline station
- ○ a grocery store
- ○ a local school

artistic   squirm

discord   talent   individual

performance

carefree

1

_____

2

_____

3

_____

4

_____

Teacher: Read aloud the vocabulary words. Have students look at each picture and write the vocabulary word that best describes it. Ask students which word they wrote under each picture and why.

Listen. Read. Write.

1

Maria is very **artistic**. She loves to draw and paint
_____ pictures.

useful

beautiful

tasty

2

Don felt **carefree** on Saturday because he planned
to play with his friends all day. "You look very
_____ today," Mom said.

bored

cheerful

lazy

3

There was **discord** when the family tried to plan
their trip. They couldn't _____
on where they should go.

agree

eat

play

4

After the students practiced reading their poems,
they gave a **performance**. Everyone enjoyed the
_____.

show

dinner

gifts

5

All of Megan's friends have dogs and cats for
pets. To show she is an **individual**, Megan wants
a _____ kind of pet.

cute

playful

different

Teacher: Read aloud each pair of sentences. Have students read the word choices and
write the best word to fill in the blank. Ask students which words they chose and why.

19

Listen. Read. Write.

1

A Strange _____ Show

Pete's class was planning a show. Everyone would share something different that they were good at doing. When the day arrived, Steve showed how to make a paper hat. Leslie got her hamster to jump through a hoop. The show was a big hit!

Talent

Squirm

Carefree

2

A _____ Day

Jessie woke up and looked at the clock on a cold winter morning. "Oh no!" she said. "I am late for school." She started to jump out of bed. Just then, Jessie's mom called up the stairs, "There's no school today. It is snowing." Jessie snuggled back into bed. She opened the book from the table beside her bed and started to read. It felt so good to have the whole day to do just as she pleased.

3

"I'LL NAME HIM _____ !"

Max's playful new puppy needed a name. "What will I call you?" said Max. The puppy kept wiggling and jiggling and twisting and turning in his arms. All of a sudden, Max said, "I know what I can call you!"

Teacher: Read aloud the vocabulary words at the top of the page. Have students read the stories and write a vocabulary word to complete each title. Ask students which words they chose to complete the titles and why.

Show What You Know

Listen. Fill in the bubble.

1 What would make you **squirm**?
- ○ lying on a beach blanket on the sand
- ○ sitting on a hard wooden bench
- ○ standing outside on a sunny day

2 What would make you feel **carefree**?
- ○ losing your homework
- ○ feeding your pet dog
- ○ having all your chores done

3 Which one is a **talent**?
- ○ eating healthy foods
- ○ having beautiful eyes
- ○ playing softball well

4 What might cause **discord**?
- ○ playing a guitar that is cracked
- ○ hanging something heavy on a rope
- ○ seeing your favorite food on a menu

5 What might an **artistic** person do?
- ○ decorate her room
- ○ keep his desk neat
- ○ put together a puzzle

6 Which one is a kind of **performance**?
- ○ doing a science experiment
- ○ humming a tune to yourself
- ○ playing drums at a talent show

7 Which action shows that Sarah is an **individual**?
- ○ She learned how to ride a bike.
- ○ She named her dog Kitty.
- ○ She wore sneakers to school like the other kids.

Listen. Read. Write.

1 Melissa **envied** Mark because he had won a free ticket to the show. Melissa said, "I _____ I had one, too."

know

think

wish

2 Ms. Boyd's class showed their **originality** by making sculptures out of milk cartons. They made many new and _____ things.

different

easy

fast

3 Pete loved **vibrant** colors. Even his toothbrush was a _____ lemon yellow.

bright

large

pale

4 Bob was **reluctant** to get up from his favorite chair. He was _____ that his brother would plop down on it.

afraid

pleased

lucky

5 Joyce wanted a **stylish** new outfit. She chose a shirt that was in fashion and looked really _____ on her.

baggy

strange

good

Teacher: Read aloud each pair of sentences. Have students read the word choices and write the best word to fill in the blank. Ask students which words they chose and why.

Listen. Read. Write.

retreat

exhausted

originality

back off

different

no energy

leave

unusual

go

interesting

run away

new

sleepy

tired

worn out

Teacher: Read aloud the vocabulary words that appear on the pajamas. Have students read the words on the stacked clothes and write each word under its related vocabulary word. Ask students which words they wrote on each pair of pajamas and why.

23

Listen. Write.

vibrant   stylish   reluctant
retreat   envy   exhausted
originality

1

2

3

4

Teacher: Read aloud the vocabulary words.
Have students look at each picture and write the
vocabulary word that best describes it. Ask students
which word they wrote under each picture and why.

24

1 Which color is **vibrant**?
- ○ bright red
- ○ light pink
- ○ gray

2 Which might cause a cat to **retreat**?
- ○ a cat toy
- ○ a mean dog
- ○ a tasty snack

3 Which would probably make you **exhausted**?
- ○ raking leaves in a really big yard
- ○ taking a long afternoon nap
- ○ talking to a good friend

4 Which person might you **envy**?
- ○ a boy whose bike had a flat tire
- ○ a child who got to take a fun trip
- ○ a family member who has a bad cold

5 What would be most **stylish**?
- ○ an old shirt that has stains on it
- ○ pants that are too short for you
- ○ a new jacket that fits just right

6 Which kind of sandwich shows the most **originality**?
- ○ grilled cheese on white bread
- ○ potato chip and jelly on a tortilla
- ○ hamburger on a toasted bun

7 Which would most people be **reluctant** to do?
- ○ play a game with friends
- ○ have a poisonous snake as a pet
- ○ take a walk in the park

Teacher: Read aloud each numbered item and have students fill in the bubble next to the correct answer.

25

1 Juanita opened the nicely decorated box. She was **astonished** by what she found inside.

_____

_____

astonished

2 Ted wanted to hang his picture on the refrigerator, but he couldn't find any magnets. "You can **anchor** it with tape," said Mom.

_____

_____

anchor

3 Ling and her friend wanted to ride their bikes, but they couldn't play outside. The weather was too **blustery**.

blustery

_____

_____

Teacher: Read aloud each numbered item. Have students write the vocabulary word under the picture that shows its meaning. Ask students which picture they chose and why.

26

Listen. Read. Write.

Blustery

Treacherous

Strive

1

_____ to Do Your Best!

Lynn wrote a story and showed it to her best friend, Vicki. "It's perfect!" Vicki said. Lynn was not happy, though. Vicki didn't laugh very much at the funny part. So Lynn worked hard to improve her story. The next time she read it aloud, Vicki laughed at the funny part.

2

A _____ Day

Whoosh! Suddenly a big puff of wind picked up a leaf and blew it through the air. Whee! Up it went over houses and across a river. Then all at once, the wind turned around and blew the leaf in a different direction, high over a playground. When the wind stopped blowing, the leaf drifted toward the ground. It settled under a tree, back where it had started.

3

THE _____ RiDE

Mr. Lee and his family went for a drive in the mountains. The higher they went, the rockier and narrower the road became. When they peered over the edge into the valley below, they were scared. Finally, they made it to the other side of the mountain.

Teacher: Read aloud the vocabulary words at the top of the page. Have students read the stories and write a vocabulary word to complete each title. Ask students which words they chose to complete the titles and why.

Listen. Write.

1.

_____

2.

_____

3.

_____

4.

_____

Teacher: Read aloud the vocabulary words. Have students look at each picture and write the vocabulary word that best describes it. Ask students which word they wrote under each picture and why.

28

1 What might happen to your umbrella on a **blustery** day?
- ○ it might blow away
- ○ it might become faded
- ○ it might get misplaced

2 Which might a **defiant** person say?
- ○ "Hello!"
- ○ "Help!"
- ○ "No!"

3 What does an **anchored** boat do?
- ○ dry out
- ○ move fast
- ○ stay in one place

4 Which would most likely make someone feel **astonished**?
- ○ a cat that could sing
- ○ a parrot that could say "Hello"
- ○ a dog that could roll over

5 What would be most **treacherous**?
- ○ a book on the floor
- ○ a puzzle piece under the bed
- ○ a toy car on the stairs

6 What might a person who is **striving** to do something say?
- ○ "This is hard, but I am going to do it anyway."
- ○ "This is too hard. Someone else can do it."
- ○ "I don't see why anyone would want to do this."

7 Which would be an **ominous** thing to see?
- ○ a friendly clown
- ○ a sleepy boy
- ○ an unhappy teacher

Teacher: Read aloud each numbered item and have students fill in the bubble next to the correct answer.

29

1 It was a rainy day. Pam and
Diane decided to make fun hats.
They used paper,
glitter, glue, and
beads. Mom
laughed, "These
are real **creations**!"

creations

2 Pat and Lee did
everything together.
They were in the same
class and played on
the same softball team
after school. People
said that they even
resembled each other.

resembled

3 A toad noticed that
a hungry turtle was
watching him. "A
disguise will keep
me from being that
turtle's lunch,"
thought the toad.

disguise

Teacher: Read aloud each numbered item. Have students write the
vocabulary word under the picture that shows its meaning. Ask students
which picture they chose and why.

Listen. Read. Write.

smear

pretend

admire

cover
fake
imagine
like

make-believe
play
respect
rub

spread
value
wipe
honor

Teacher: Read aloud the vocabulary words that appear on each slice of bread. Have students read the words on the jars and write each word under its related vocabulary word. Ask students which words they wrote on each slice of bread and why.

Listen. Read. Write.

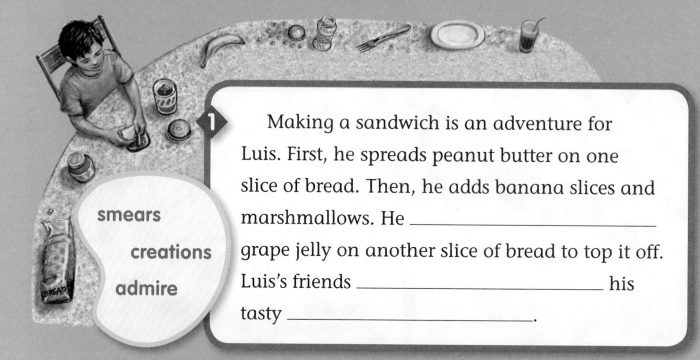

smears

creations

admire

1 Making a sandwich is an adventure for Luis. First, he spreads peanut butter on one slice of bread. Then, he adds banana slices and marshmallows. He _____ grape jelly on another slice of bread to top it off. Luis's friends _____ his tasty _____.

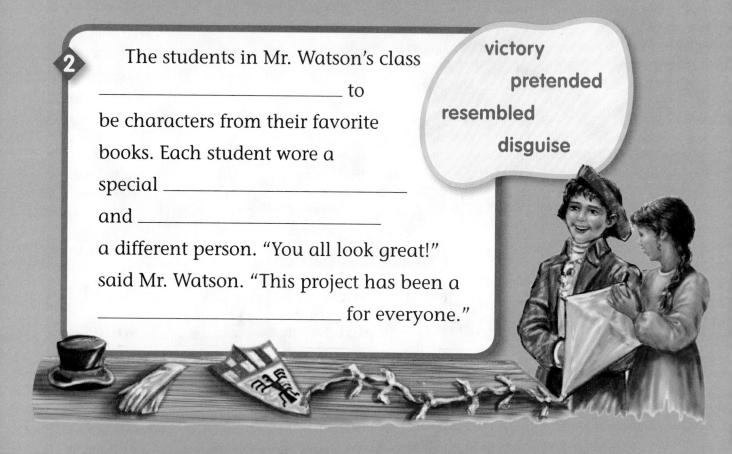

victory

pretended

resembled

disguise

2 The students in Mr. Watson's class _____ to be characters from their favorite books. Each student wore a special _____ and _____ a different person. "You all look great!" said Mr. Watson. "This project has been a _____ for everyone."

Teacher: Read aloud the vocabulary words in the shapes. Then have students read the stories and write the best words to fill in the blanks. Ask students which words they chose to complete each story and why.

1 What would you **admire** someone for?
- ○ being in a bad mood
- ○ hearing a bird sing
- ○ telling the truth

2 What might you **smear** on a cake?
- ○ frosting
- ○ paint
- ○ plastic wrap

3 What would you say to someone about her **victory**?
- ○ "I'm sorry that you didn't win."
- ○ "I am happy for you!"
- ○ "Keep trying."

4 Which would most likely be part of a **disguise**?
- ○ a belt
- ○ a mask
- ○ a wallet

5 What could you **pretend** to be?
- ○ a child
- ○ an astronaut
- ○ a student

6 Which would be a **creation**?
- ○ a black crayon
- ○ a raw potato
- ○ a sand castle

7 Which might **resemble** a wolf?
- ○ a dog
- ○ a lion
- ○ a snake

Teacher: Read aloud each numbered item and have students fill in the bubble next to the correct answer.

33

Long ago, there were no sports. Instead, people watched contests in which knights on horses battled each other. One day Sir Nigel and Sir Trevor met in such a contest. The sun was high above the place where the earth and sky meet. The two knights rode to opposite ends of the field and then turned to face each other. Suddenly they lifted their spears and their horses charged. Whoosh! Sir Trevor struck the enemy, knocking him off his horse. Sir Nigel lay on the ground with his arms and legs spread out as the winner pranced around the field. The outcome was clear. Sir Nigel limped away, upset that he had lost the contest.

obvious
defeat
sprawled
bout
horizon

1 Sir Nigel and Sir Trevor were knights who fought a _____.

2 The sun was high above the _____.

3 Sir Nigel _____ on the ground after he was knocked from his horse.

4 It was _____ that Sir Trevor had won the contest.

5 Sir Nigel was upset at his _____ at the hands of Sir Trevor.

Teacher: Have students read the story. Then read the vocabulary words aloud. Have students read the sentences and write the vocabulary word that best completes each sentence. Ask students which words they wrote and why.

34

Listen. Write.

1

_____

2

_____

3

_____

4

_____

Teacher: Read aloud the vocabulary words. Have students look at each picture and write the vocabulary word that best describes it. Ask students which word they wrote under each picture and why.

35

Listen. Read. Write.

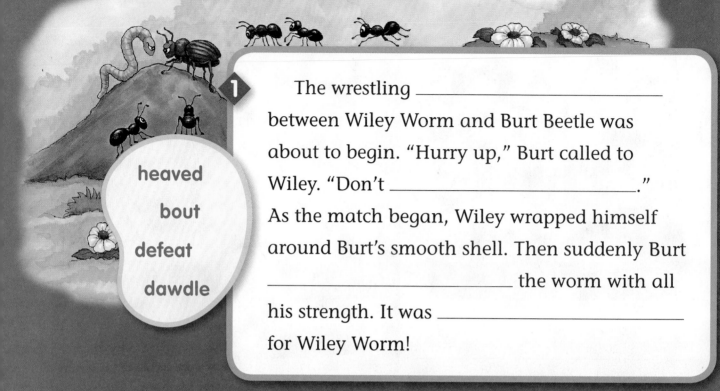

1

heaved

bout

defeat

dawdle

The wrestling _____ between Wiley Worm and Burt Beetle was about to begin. "Hurry up," Burt called to Wiley. "Don't _____."
As the match began, Wiley wrapped himself around Burt's smooth shell. Then suddenly Burt _____ the worm with all his strength. It was _____ for Wiley Worm!

2

Ray and his friends looked toward the _____ just as the sun was setting. They had just eaten and were _____ out beside the campfire. It was _____ that the boys were exhausted from their long hike in the woods.

horizon

sprawled

obvious

Teacher: Read aloud the vocabulary words in the shapes. Then have students read each story and write the best words to fill in the blanks. Ask students which words they chose to complete each story and why.

Show What You Know

Listen. Fill in the bubble.

1 What could happen in a **bout**?
- ○ someone gets lost
- ○ someone sleeps
- ○ someone wins

2 What could you see on the **horizon**?
- ○ the rug
- ○ the sun
- ○ the mirror

3 Where would a person **sprawl**?
- ○ in a sink
- ○ on a bike
- ○ on a bed

4 Which person might be **defeated**?
- ○ a runner in a race
- ○ a clerk in a store
- ○ a clown on television

5 What might you **heave**?
- ○ a mountain
- ○ a glass vase
- ○ a heavy backpack

6 What would be **obvious** if you looked in the mirror?
- ○ that your left foot hurt
- ○ that your nose was sunburned
- ○ that you had a headache

7 What might you say to someone who **dawdles**?
- ○ "Get moving or you'll be late!"
- ○ "Good job!"
- ○ "Slow down, you're moving too fast!"

1 Jill used her scissors to make a **spiral** out of pink ribbon. She then used the ribbon to make a _____ bow for the gift she was wrapping.

straight

curly

short

2 Band music floated through the air as the **ceremony** began. The _____ honored the city's new mayor.

event

problem

class

3 I was so hungry that I ate some **stale** bread. It was very dry and hard, and it tasted really _____.

bad

sweet

salty

4 Dad was **disgusted** by Dan's messy room. He was _____ about the dirty clothes on the floor.

proud

delighted

upset

5 The bright January sunshine **deceived** us. It made us believe that it was _____ outside.

rainy

warm

cold

Teacher: Read aloud each pair of sentences. Have students read the word choices and write the best word to fill in the blank. Ask students which words they chose and why.

Listen. Read. Write.

1

The _____ *Staircase*

The staircase was unlike anything we had ever seen because the steps did not go up in a straight line. They wrapped around a large pole, circling up and up. Climbing the stairs was like riding a spinning top.

2

A _____ **Treat**

A few days ago Jan had baked a blueberry pie, and there was one slice left. She cut into the pie with her fork. One mouthful told the story—yuck! The crust was no longer fresh. The blueberries were hard and chewy. Her special treat was spoiled!

3

_____ **and Disappointed**

We couldn't wait to go to the new theme park. Ads boasted that it had the biggest rides and the best snacks in the world. Our first stop was the roller coaster, but it was shut down. The Tilt-A-Whirl was closed for repairs. The snack hut had only old popcorn. Don't believe everything you read!

Teacher: Read aloud the vocabulary words at the top of the page. Have students read the stories and write a vocabulary word to complete each title. Ask students which words they chose to complete the titles and why.

Listen. Write.

1 The Smiths were anxious to see their newly painted living room. They were filled with **disgust** when they opened the door.

_____

disgust

_____

_____

2 Greg wanted to be class president. He worked hard to **persuade** his classmates to vote for him.

_____

persuade

3 Jenna was riding her bike when suddenly a dog ran across her path. She made an **abrupt** stop to avoid hitting the animal.

abrupt

_____

_____

Teacher: Read aloud each numbered item. Have students write the vocabulary word under the picture that shows its meaning. Ask students which picture they chose and why.

1 Which could get **stale**?
- ○ wool
- ○ bread
- ○ sand

2 What might you hear at a **ceremony**?
- ○ speeches
- ○ splashes
- ○ honking

3 Which could be **disgusting**?
- ○ a shelf of books
- ○ a pair of new shoes
- ○ a piece of moldy fruit

4 Which could make an **abrupt** sound?
- ○ waves lapping on the beach
- ○ glass breaking
- ○ a flag fluttering

5 What might a person who was **deceived** say?
- ○ "You tricked me!"
- ○ "Thanks for inviting me!"
- ○ "I am so pleased!"

6 Which one might move in a **spiral**?
- ○ a sleeping cat
- ○ a speeding train
- ○ a diving hawk

7 How could you **persuade** your friend to visit?
- ○ read a book
- ○ write a letter
- ○ go on vacation

Teacher: Read aloud each numbered item and have students fill in the bubble next to the correct answer.

display   paralyzed

orbit

warp   tilt

coincidence

achieve

1

2

_____

3

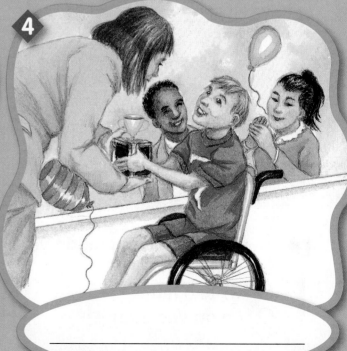

4

_____

_____

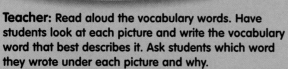

_____

Teacher: Read aloud the vocabulary words. Have
students look at each picture and write the vocabulary
word that best describes it. Ask students which word
they wrote under each picture and why.

Listen. Read. Write.

slant

order

present

set out

planet

spin

uneven

lean

go around

circle

show

tip

tilt

_____

_____

_____

_____

orbit

_____

_____

_____

_____

display

_____

_____

_____

Teacher: Read aloud the vocabulary words that appear on each spaceship. Have students read the words on the stars and planets and write each word under its related vocabulary word. Ask students which words they wrote on each spaceship and why.

43

This was Shelly's first skateboard contest. A huge skating ramp stood in the center of the park. At the bottom of the ramp, the wood had been bent and twisted so that it curved. Shelly had never ridden such a big ramp. Could she do her very best and win the prize? The first round began. For a minute, Shelly was frozen with fear at the top of the ramp. She tipped her board over the side. Soon she was diving and flying, up and down the ramp. Before she knew it, the round was over. Shelly had won first place! And to her surprise, Shelly's best friend Lisa had finished second. Both girls smiled as they accepted their prizes.

achieve

coincidence

paralyzed

tilted

warped

1 The wood at the bottom of the ramp was _____.

2 Shelly wanted to _____ in the contest.

3 At first Shelly felt _____ on the ramp.

4 Shelly _____ her skateboard over the edge.

5 It was a _____ that both Shelly and Lisa won prizes in the same contest.

Teacher: Have students read the story. Then read the vocabulary words aloud. Have students read the sentences and write the word that best completes each sentence. Ask students which words they wrote and why.

1 When is a time you might feel **paralyzed**?
- ○ at home reading a book
- ○ at the top of a roller coaster
- ○ building a snowman

2 What would you be likely to see in a store window **display**?
- ○ orange peels, eggshells, stale cheese
- ○ rubber bands, keys, broken pencils
- ○ dresses, hats, shoes

3 What might seem like a time **warp**?
- ○ a cold rainstorm
- ○ a short phone call
- ○ a long airplane ride

4 What moves in an **orbit**?
- ○ insects
- ○ planets
- ○ clouds

5 When does a **coincidence** occur?
- ○ when something falls apart
- ○ when two things happen at once
- ○ when someone forgets something

6 If you **tilt** a cup of water, what will happen?
- ○ water will pour
- ○ water will leak
- ○ water will freeze

7 If you want to **achieve**, what do you have to do?
- ○ take a short rest
- ○ change all the rules
- ○ try your very best

Teacher: Read aloud each numbered item and have students fill in the bubble next to the correct answer.

45

Listen. Write.

1 The bus was crowded, and many people were standing. Beth could remain seated or let someone else take her seat. She chose to be **gracious**.

gracious

2 Jake's class was taking a tour of Old Town. Suddenly Jake noticed an **inscription** on an old building. "This place was built in 1887," he called out to his classmates.

inscription

3 **Diplomats** talk with leaders from different countries. They try to solve problems in a way that brings peace.

diplomat

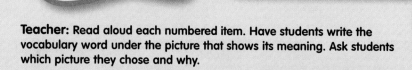

Teacher: Read aloud each numbered item. Have students write the vocabulary word under the picture that shows its meaning. Ask students which picture they chose and why.

Listen. Read. Write.

1 My friend is very **humane**. She is known for her _____ treatment of animals.

kind
fun
cold

2 Red flashing lights **indicate** danger. They show that there _____ something to watch out for.

is not
could be
is

3 Julio wanted to **confirm** that his flight was on time. He called the airline to _____ what time the plane would take off.

check
remember
warn

4 Richard could barely read the **inscription** on the old wall. The _____ had almost worn off.

smell
heat
writing

5 My teacher has a lot of **integrity**. She is always _____ and treats everyone with kindness.

quick
fair
nervous

Listen. Read. Write.

1

The crowd clapped when the _____ stood up to speak. He read the _____ on the new monument that the _____ citizens had built. Then he spoke of the _____ of the heroes they honored that day.

inscription

gracious

integrity

diplomat

2   I called ahead to _____ Rusty's appointment with Dr. Green, our veterinarian. Dr. Green is known for her _____ treatment of animals. Her gentle way with pets _____ her love for animals.

humane

confirm

indicates

1 What might **indicate** that someone is at the front door?
- ○ a TV show
- ○ a phone call
- ○ the doorbell

2 Where could you find an **inscription**?
- ○ on a car seat
- ○ in your closet
- ○ on a bridge

3 How would you **confirm** if it was raining?
- ○ look for your coat
- ○ look outside
- ○ read a book

4 Which one is **humane**?
- ○ someone who helps get homes painted
- ○ someone who likes to take walks
- ○ someone who helps cats find homes

5 What is one job of a **diplomat**?
- ○ to make peace
- ○ to make pizza
- ○ to fly in airplanes

6 Who has **integrity**?
- ○ someone who doesn't win
- ○ someone who doesn't lie
- ○ someone who doesn't cook

7 Why is it fun to visit someone who is **gracious**?
- ○ that person is nice
- ○ that person is clean
- ○ that person will call

Teacher: Read aloud each numbered item and have students fill in the bubble next to the correct answer.

49

1

The _____ Boy

Ambitious

Mischievous

Sympathy

Brian likes to play tricks on people. He might place a rubber snake on a chair, leap out at someone, or make a scary noise. When people jump or scream in fright, Brian rolls with laughter.

2

_____ in Action

Nate is one of the kindest and most thoughtful boys in his class. Everyone calls him "Nice Nate" because he often goes out of his way to help others. One night each week Nate brings meals to people in his community who cannot cook for themselves.

3

_____ Plans

Maurice has always been determined to accomplish great things. Sometimes his parents think that his goals are too high, but Maurice usually succeeds. Whether he's shooting baskets or writing a report, Maurice tries hard to do his best.

Teacher: Read aloud the vocabulary words at the top of the page. Have students read the stories and write a vocabulary word to complete each title. Ask students which words they chose to complete the titles and why.

Listen. Read. Write.

glance

common

playful

usual

naughty

check

regular

fun-loving

scan

familiar

look at

skim

mischievous

ordinary

sly

Teacher: Read aloud the vocabulary words that appear on each pen. Have students read the words on the sheep and write each word under its related vocabulary word. Ask students which words they wrote in each pen and why.

Listen. Write.

ordinary   sympathy   scan

scowl   mischievous   ambitious

apology

1

_____

2

_____

3

_____

4

_____

Teacher: Read aloud the vocabulary words. Have students look at each picture and write the vocabulary word that best describes it. Ask students which word they wrote under each picture and why.

52

1 Which would be an **ordinary** after-school outfit?
- ○ blue jeans and a T-shirt
- ○ a lacy gown with glass slippers
- ○ a black silk cape with a top hat

2 What might make you **scowl**?
- ○ being told you have to stay after school
- ○ being told you have won an award
- ○ being told you are a hard worker

3 Which person is **mischievous**?
- ○ someone who plays ball
- ○ someone who plays the piano
- ○ someone who plays tricks

4 What might you see if you **scanned** a beach?
- ○ salt air and cool breezes
- ○ sea gulls and sand castles
- ○ different shapes of sand grains

5 Which is an example of an **apology**?
- ○ "Please pass the salt."
- ○ "Thank you for coming."
- ○ "I'm sorry to be late."

6 Who is an **ambitious** person?
- ○ someone who wants to win
- ○ someone who wants to sleep late
- ○ someone who wants to help out

7 To whom might you show **sympathy**?
- ○ a person who has many friends
- ○ a person who is ungrateful to friends
- ○ a person who has lost a close friend

Teacher: Read aloud each numbered item and have students fill in the bubble next to the correct answer.

Cayla and Jade glided around the ice rink. Both girls hoped to win medals in tonight's skating event. Suddenly Jade leaped into the air and landed hard on the ice, twisting her ankle as she fell. Cayla skated quickly to her side.

"My foot hurts—a lot," groaned Jade, as Cayla bent over to comfort her friend. Jade's coach hurried over to check her leg. Then he helped Jade off the ice.

All at once Cayla noticed that the crowd of people who had come to watch the skaters were standing up, smiling at her and clapping loudly! And right in the front row was her mom with the biggest smile of all. Cayla knew then that whether she skated well or not, the most important thing was that she had helped her friend.

spectators

ovation

beaming

priority

anguish

1 Jade felt _____ when she fell.

2 A crowd of _____ were watching the skaters.

3 The crowd gave Cayla an _____.

4 Cayla's Mom was _____ because she was so proud.

5 Helping Jade was a _____ to Cayla.

Teacher: Have students read the story. Then read the vocabulary words aloud. Have students read the sentences and write the vocabulary word that best completes each sentence. Ask students which words they wrote and why.

Listen. Write.

1 Tate heard a loud squawking and splashing. He ran to the birdbath and saw a blue jay flapping angrily in the water. Just below was his cat Minnie, **poised** to leap up and grab the bird.

_____

_____

poised

_____

_____

2 Katie ran faster and faster as she approached the finish line. Suddenly she fell. Her coach quickly ran out on the track to **assist** her.

assist

3 The score was tied when Jason came up to bat. He swung hard, and the baseball flew over the outfield fence. The crowd gave their hero an **ovation**.

ovation

_____

_____

Teacher: Read aloud each numbered item. Have students write the vocabulary word under the picture that shows its meaning. Ask students which picture they chose and why.

Listen. Read. Write.

1

The **spectators** lined the streets. They were excited to _____ the big parade.

stop

watch

leave

2

Zach made his homework a **priority** every day. He did his homework _____ he played with his friends.

after

before

while

3

The runners were **poised** at the line. They were ready to _____ the race.

stop

start

end

4

The dog trainer **assisted** me in teaching my new puppy a trick. She said "I'd be happy to _____ you!"

write

stop

help

5

Mike's broken leg caused him great **anguish**. The _____ was unbearable!

pain

boredom

excitement

Teacher: Read aloud each pair of sentences. Have students read the word choices and write the best word to fill in the blank. Ask students which words they chose and why.

1 What would **spectators** do?
- ○ bake a cake
- ○ clap and cheer
- ○ read a book

2 Which one is **poised** for action?
- ○ a sleeping dog
- ○ a boy on a diving board
- ○ a girl watching TV

3 What might cause someone to feel **anguish**?
- ○ a glass of lemonade
- ○ a stubbed toe
- ○ lively music

4 Where might you hear an **ovation**?
- ○ at a fruit stand
- ○ at the circus
- ○ at a music store

5 Which person is most likely to be **beaming**?
- ○ someone who is happy
- ○ someone who is lazy
- ○ someone who is frightened

6 Which word describes someone who **assists** others?
- ○ selfish
- ○ helpful
- ○ careless

7 Which would be a **priority** for a baseball player?
- ○ eating pizza
- ○ talking on the phone
- ○ going to batting practice

Teacher: Read aloud each numbered item and have students fill in the bubble next to the correct answer.

Listen. Write.

majestic
adorn
vendor
emerald
organize
conceal
restore

1

2

3

4

Teacher: Read aloud the vocabulary words. Have students look at each picture and write the vocabulary word that best describes it. Ask students which word they wrote under each picture and why.

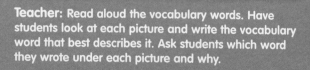

Listen. Read. Write.

adorn

organize

majestic

plan

sparkle

great

dress up

powerful

lovely

manage

grand

decorate

order

royal

sort

Teacher: Read aloud the vocabulary words that appear on each rock. Have students read the words on the lizards and write each word under its related vocabulary word. Ask students which words they wrote on each rock and why.

59

Listen. Read. Write.

1

Once there was a tired king who took a trip to the beach to _____ his energy. Every day he wore a T-shirt and shorts, since kings don't have to look _____ at the beach. Swimming in the warm _____ ocean was such great fun that he could not _____ his happiness.

majestic

conceal

restore

emerald

2

Patti set up a lemonade stand. First she made a sign and _____ the things she would need. Then she mixed two pitchers of lemonade and _____ the table with bright flowers. After selling her first glass of lemonade, Patti declared, "Now I am a real _____!"

vendor

organized

adorned

Teacher: Read aloud the vocabulary words in the shapes. Then have students read the stories and write the best words to fill in the blanks. Ask students which words they chose to complete each story and why.

60

1 What could you **organize**?
- ○ cereal in a box
- ○ dishes in a cupboard
- ○ water in a tub

2 What might you ask a **vendor**?
- ○ "Do you have a brother or sister?"
- ○ "How much does this cost?"
- ○ "What do I have to do for homework?"

3 Which is **emerald**-colored?
- ○ the inside of a lemon
- ○ the outside of a watermelon
- ○ the skin of a peach

4 Which would you **adorn** an ice-cream sundae with?
- ○ a cherry
- ○ a scoop of ice cream
- ○ a spoon

5 Which animal is most **majestic**?
- ○ a kitten
- ○ a lion
- ○ a mouse

6 What might you say if you were **restoring** a bike?
- ○ "I do not have enough money to buy this."
- ○ "It is not safe to ride this on the street."
- ○ "I will give it a new coat of paint."

7 Which animal can **conceal** itself with a body part?
- ○ a crab
- ○ a dog
- ○ a turtle

Listen. Write.

1 Bob was upset. His brother Stan kept taking his trucks to play with without asking him. Finally the boys solved their problem in a **mature** way.

_____

_____

mature

_____

2 Dad took Ann to the animal shelter to pick out a pet. Ann looked at several kittens. Finally she chose a **frisky** one.

_____

frisky

3 The sun went down and the air got cool. Tom's family **huddled** under a blanket near the campfire and told stories.

_____

huddled

_____

Teacher: Read aloud each numbered item. Have students write the vocabulary word under the picture that shows its meaning. Ask students which picture they chose and why.

Listen. Read. Write.

1 Every morning Farmer Dell has to get up early to let the horses into a field to **graze**. "These guys sure like to _____," he laughs.

eat
play
run

2 Ying knew that she would have to **adapt** when she moved to the United States from China. Much about her life would _____.

buy
change
see

3 The baby started to cry, so Grandma picked her up to **soothe** her. After a few minutes, the baby was _____.

hungry
mad
quiet

4 José was **determined** to win the big race. There was _____ that anyone could do to stop him.

nothing
something
little

5 The penguins **huddled** against the cold wind. They moved _____ and formed a tight circle.

apart
down
together

Teacher: Read aloud each pair of sentences. Have students read the word choices and write the best word to fill in the blank. Ask students which words they chose and why.

63

Elephants never forget—except for young Eddie. Thoughts just slipped from his memory like a breeze through the jungle trees. Eddie's mom tried to comfort her son, but that didn't help. So Eddie decided to visit the lion, the wisest animal in the jungle.

Eddie set out early the next morning. He passed a group of hippos standing close together near the edge of a river. He spotted a herd of zebras munching grass in an open area. Finally he reached the lion's den. The lion listened to Eddie's story.

"Until your memory gets stronger, you must make some changes," said the lion, as he tied a string around Eddie's trunk. "This string will help you remember." Now Eddie would never forget.

determined

graze

soothe

huddle

adapt

1 Eddie's mom tries to _____ him.

2 Eddie is _____ to visit the lion.

3 The hippos _____ at the edge of the river.

4 The zebras _____ in an open area.

5 The string will help Eddie _____ until his memory gets stronger.

Teacher: Have students read the story. Then read the vocabulary words aloud. Have students read the sentences and write the vocabulary word that best completes each sentence. Ask students which words they wrote and why.

1 Which would you **huddle** with?
- ○ friends
- ○ flowers
- ○ toys

2 How is a **mature** animal different from a baby one?
- ○ It's bigger.
- ○ It's friendlier.
- ○ It's softer.

3 What might someone have to **adapt** to?
- ○ a best friend
- ○ a favorite food
- ○ a new school

4 Which animal is most likely to be **frisky**?
- ○ a dog
- ○ a starfish
- ○ a worm

5 What might a **determined** person say?
- ○ "I might be able to win the contest."
- ○ "I am sure I will win the contest."
- ○ "I doubt that I will win the contest."

6 Which would be a **soothing** thing to say?
- ○ "Are you hungry?"
- ○ "Don't be scared."
- ○ "I love chocolate."

7 Where might an animal **graze**?
- ○ in a field
- ○ on the beach
- ○ in a desert

Teacher: Read aloud each numbered item and have students fill in the bubble next to the correct answer.

Diligent

Gentle

Pesky

1

THE _____ INSECT

Glance at any flower garden and
you'll probably spot a colorful butterfly.
Its paper-thin wings lift it ever so
lightly from bloom to bloom. The insect
touches down softly on one flower and
then floats along to its next landing place.

2

THE _____ INSECT

Flies are drawn to picnics like nails are drawn
to magnets. These insects land on your hot dogs
and slosh through the sweet, sticky juice of your
watermelon. Brush flies away, and they're soon
back again. So the next time you plan a picnic,
be prepared to share it with some tiny pests.

3

The _____ Insect

A bee's work never seems to end. Bees travel from
one bloom to another sucking up liquid. When the
sack in their body is full, they return to the hive,
where they store this liquid in wax cells. Bees also
clean and guard the hive and care for the young.
Some bees even become builders that make and
repair wax cells. A bee's life is all work and no play.

Teacher: Read aloud the vocabulary words at the top of the page. Have students read the stories and write a
vocabulary word to complete each title. Ask students which words they chose to complete the titles and why.

Listen. Read. Write.

trick

loving

doze

fool

confuse

mild

rest

trap

kind

nap

tame

sleep

gentle

outsmart

slumber

Teacher: Read aloud the vocabulary words that appear on each basket. Have students read the words on the apples and write each word under its related vocabulary word. Ask students which words they wrote on each basket and why.

67

Listen. Write.

gentle   abundant   pesky
idle   slumber
diligent
outsmart

1

_____

2

_____

3

_____

4

_____

Teacher: Read aloud the vocabulary words. Have
students look at each picture and write the vocabulary
word that best describes it. Ask students which word
they wrote under each picture and why.

68

1 Which needs to be handled in a **gentle** way?
- ○ a refrigerator
- ○ a garbage truck
- ○ a tiny baby

2 Which is an **abundant** amount of corn for a family meal?
- ○ a basketful
- ○ a plateful
- ○ a spoonful

3 Which animal is the most likely to be **pesky**?
- ○ a cow
- ○ a turtle
- ○ a puppy

4 When is the best time to **slumber**?
- ○ in the morning on the bus
- ○ at night after a long day
- ○ in the afternoon during work

5 What does someone who is **idle** do?
- ○ cleans the house
- ○ runs errands
- ○ sits on the couch

6 What does it take to be a **diligent** person?
- ○ hard work and seriousness
- ○ patience and a sense of humor
- ○ kindness and understanding

7 Which words describe someone who can **outsmart** others?
- ○ gentle and kind
- ○ clever and creative
- ○ stubborn and selfish

Teacher: Read aloud each numbered item and have students fill in the bubble next to the correct answer.

69

mail

weak

rough

hurtful

enjoy

thank

hard

mean

skinny

bony

thin

prize

treasure

scrawny

appreciate

harsh

Teacher: Read aloud the vocabulary words that appear on each mailbox. Have students read the words on the letters and write each word under its related vocabulary word. Ask students which words they wrote on each mailbox and why.

Listen. Read. Write.

embarrass

confidence

harsh

1   Todd really tried never to tease or
_____ his sister
Anita. He didn't use any words that
sounded _____.
They might hurt Anita's feelings. Todd
only said things that would build up
his sister's _____.

2   Anita tried with all of her might to draw a
_____ squirrel
for her science project, but the result
was _____.
Todd figured that his sister might
_____ some
help. He showed Anita how to change the
squirrel's _____ tail to a
bushy one with a few strokes of her paintbrush.

appreciate

dreadful   scrawny

perfect

Teacher: Read aloud the vocabulary words in the shapes. Then have students read each passage and write the best words to fill in the blanks. Ask students which words they chose to complete each passage and why.

71

The sun shone brightly against the clear blue sky on the opening day of the state fair. Adam had been looking forward to this day all year.

Adam enjoyed everything about the fair, but he was most excited about riding the roller coaster. Last year he had been too small to ride. "You are too thin and weak to hang on," the ride operator had said, laughing. Adam remembered feeling silly as he walked away.

This year Adam walked up to the roller coaster feeling good about himself. He was much bigger and stronger than before. But after 20 minutes of waiting in line, Adam noticed some low, dark clouds moving in. Soon sheets of heavy rain poured down, and everyone ran for cover. To Adam, the situation could not have been any worse.

embarrassed

confident

dreadful

perfect

scrawny

1 The weather was _____.

2 The last time Adam tried to ride the roller coaster, the ride operator said he was _____.

3 Adam was _____ when the ride operator turned him away.

4 Adam felt _____ when he walked up to the roller coaster this time.

5 Adam felt _____ about the change in the weather.

Teacher: Have students read the story. Then read the vocabulary words aloud. Have students read the sentences and write the word that best completes each sentence. Ask students which words they wrote and why.

1 Which of the following would earn you a **perfect** test score?
- ○ no wrong answers
- ○ some wrong answers
- ○ all wrong answers

2 What might you do for someone whom you **appreciate**?
- ○ give him a gift
- ○ play a trick on him
- ○ make fun of him

3 Which mistake might be **dreadful**?
- ○ leaving your socks in the bathroom
- ○ misspelling a word in a story you are writing
- ○ throwing away your favorite shoes

4 What might an animal that is **scrawny** look like?
- ○ plump and round
- ○ thin and bony
- ○ soft and furry

5 What action might **embarrass** a person?
- ○ drinking a glass of milk
- ○ eating too many chips
- ○ dropping a lunch tray

6 What might give you **confidence**?
- ○ being asked to show the class something you do well
- ○ being sent to the nurse's office
- ○ being told to listen carefully

7 What might you do if the weather were **harsh**?
- ○ have a picnic at the park
- ○ ride your bike to the store
- ○ stay home and read a good book

Teacher: Read aloud each numbered item and have students fill in the bubble next to the correct answer.

73

1

_____ PAYS OFF

Disappointed

Faded

Patience

A bright orange T-shirt lay on a shelf in a department store for a year. It waited and waited for someone to buy it. The shirt never became sad. It was sure that someday someone would buy it. The next day, someone did.

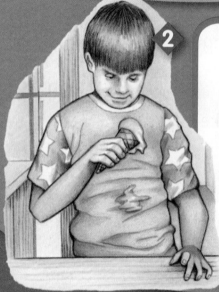

2

A _____ Favorite

Billy's favorite T-shirt was the dark blue one with white stars. It got dirty every time Billy wore it, so into the washing machine it went. With all the wearing and washing, the T-shirt soon began to lose its color. Before long, it was a lighter shade of blue, but it was still Billy's favorite.

3

The _____ T-shirt

Sally won a yellow T-shirt in a bike race. She wanted to wash the shirt but didn't read the directions. She washed it in hot soapy water and then dried it in a hot dryer. She took the T-shirt out of the dryer and saw that it had shrunk to half its size. The T-shirt was very upset. It knew Sally would never wear it now.

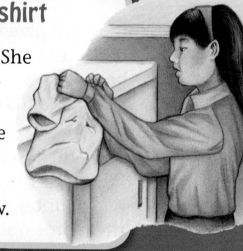

Teacher: Read aloud the vocabulary words at the top of the page. Have students read the stories and write a vocabulary word to complete each title. Ask students which words they chose to complete the titles and why.

Listen. Read. Write

1   Marla had been _____ the school party for weeks. She waited with _____ to wear her new red dress. The day before the party, Marla's mother washed her dress. To her horror, its bright red color _____ to pink. Marla had never felt so _____.

disappointed

faded

anticipating

patience

2   Bruce and his father hiked along a stream that _____ its way through the woods. Suddenly the trail led into a grassy _____ filled with bright yellow flowers. Bruce and his father loved being outdoors. The beauty of nature filled them with _____.

threaded

meadow   awe

Teacher: Read aloud the vocabulary words in the shapes. Then have students read the stories and write the best words to fill in the blanks. Ask students which words they chose to complete each story and why.

Cara and her family had set up their tent in a grassy field near a stream. Cara had awakened hours before her family. She went outside and sat on a nearby log, waiting for sunrise. Cara knew the day would have some wonderful things in store. Soon birds began chirping and leaves started rustling.

Cara spotted a small garter snake weaving in and out between some tall clumps of grass. As the sun slowly grew brighter, the moon turned paler and paler. Cara sighed and enjoyed the beauty that was around her.

1 Cara and her family set up their tent in the _____.

2 Cara sat on a log and was _____.

3 Cara _____ the upcoming day.

4 The snake _____ through the grass.

5 The moon _____ as the sun came up.

anticipated
threaded
meadow
faded
patient

Teacher: Have students read the story. Then read the vocabulary words aloud. Have students read the sentences and write the vocabulary word that best completes each sentence. Ask students which words they wrote and why.

1 What might make a brightly colored shirt **fade**?
- ○ washing it many times
- ○ wearing it under a jacket
- ○ removing its buttons

2 What might make someone **disappointed**?
- ○ getting lots of gifts
- ○ getting sick on a special day
- ○ getting a party invitation

3 Which of the following might **thread** through a neighborhood?
- ○ a large oak tree
- ○ a busy shopping center
- ○ a winding bike path

4 What might you find in a **meadow**?
- ○ sand and shells
- ○ insects and wildflowers
- ○ cars and buildings

5 What might someone with a lot of **patience** do?
- ○ eat while they are walking
- ○ interrupt someone while they are talking
- ○ wait calmly in a long line

6 What might someone feeling **awe** say?
- ○ "This is amazing!"
- ○ "This is boring."
- ○ "This is silly!"

7 Which might someone **anticipate**?
- ○ riding in a car all day
- ○ washing the family car
- ○ buying a new car

Teacher: Read aloud each numbered item and have students fill in the bubble next to the correct answer.

magnificent   variety

overrun   imaginative

disaster

pursue

bizarre

1

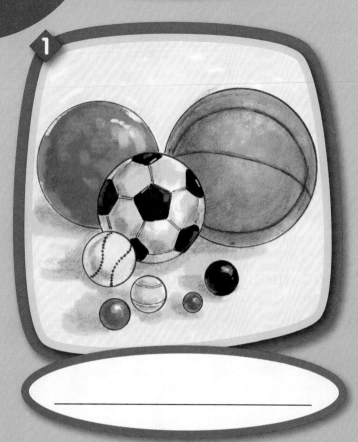

_____

2

_____

3

_____

4

_____

Teacher: Read aloud the vocabulary words. Have students look at each picture and write the vocabulary word that best describes it. Ask students which word they wrote under each picture and why.

Listen. Read. Write.

1 Mrs. Wong wanted to paint her house in a **variety** of colors. At the store, she bought many _____ colors of paint.

different

bright

silly

2 The earthquake was quite a **disaster**. Many people's homes were _____.

saved

ruined

useful

3 The town was **overrun** with people who were on their way to the festival. Never had the place been so _____.

free

pretty

crowded

4 Writing **imaginative** stories and poems is one of Sandy's favorite hobbies. She has a lot of very _____ ideas.

simple

interesting

boring

5 The hikers had a **magnificent** view from the cliff. They felt awe at the _____ of the scene.

silence

beauty

motion

Teacher: Read aloud each pair of sentences. Have students read the word choices and write the best word to fill in the blank. Ask students which words they chose and why.

79

Listen. Read. Write.

Magnificent

Bizarre

Pursue

1

A _____ Dog

Cindy has a tiny dog named Zoo. Zoo is not like other dogs. He can squeak like a gerbil. He loves to eat cat food, not dog food. He even likes to sit on Cindy's shoulder like a parrot. "I named him Zoo because he is like having many different animals in one," Cindy says.

2

_____ !

Todd made up a new game. One person is the leader. He or she runs, skips, or hops. A second person chases the leader. This person has to run, skip, or hop just like the leader. The chaser wins if he or she catches the leader. If the chaser gives up, the leader wins.

3

The _____ Gift

Rhonda had always dreamed of learning to ice skate. She did not tell Mom about her wish, however. Rhonda knew that ice skates were expensive. One morning there was a big box on Rhonda's chair. Rhonda couldn't believe her eyes when she opened it. There was a pair of the most beautiful skates she had ever seen.

Teacher: Read aloud the vocabulary words at the top of the page. Have students read the stories and write a vocabulary word to complete each title. Ask students which words they chose to complete the titles and why.

80

1 Which might **overrun** a garden?
- ○ soil
- ○ water
- ○ weeds

2 Which is most **imaginative**?
- ○ a hat made from cloth
- ○ a hat made from peanuts
- ○ a hat made of plastic

3 Which would you most likely have a **variety** of?
- ○ eyeglasses
- ○ shirts
- ○ faces

4 Which would be a **disaster**?
- ○ breaking your arm
- ○ breaking an egg
- ○ breaking a pencil point

5 What might a person **pursue**?
- ○ a bird in a cage
- ○ a runaway dog
- ○ a sleeping cat

6 Which might a person say if she saw something **magnificent**?
- ○ "I want to take a picture."
- ○ "Is it lunch time?"
- ○ "Let's get out of here."

7 Which would be a **bizarre** thing for a person to do?
- ○ pet a dog
- ○ act like a dog
- ○ wash a dog

Teacher: Read aloud each numbered item and have students fill in the bubble next to the correct answer.

1 Terry made a gift for her dad. If Terry showed the gift to her little sister, she might spoil the surprise! At last, Terry decided to **reveal** the gift.

reveal

2 Ann and Tim were working hard on their science project. Tim's mom noticed the picture they had drawn. "You two are **industrious**."

industrious

3 Sometimes Will goes to the library alone. Today Julie decided to **accompany** him.

accompany

Teacher: Read aloud each numbered item. Have students write the vocabulary word under the picture that shows its meaning. Ask students which picture they chose and why.

Listen. Read. Write.

remote

_____

_____

_____

conserve

_____

_____

_____

gesture

_____

_____

_____

save

far

nod

guard

move

keep

alone

wave

protect

point

separate

apart

Teacher: Read aloud the vocabulary words that appear in the rain forest. Have students read the words on the monkeys and write each word under its related vocabulary word. Ask students which words they wrote in each area and why.

83

Listen. Read. Write.

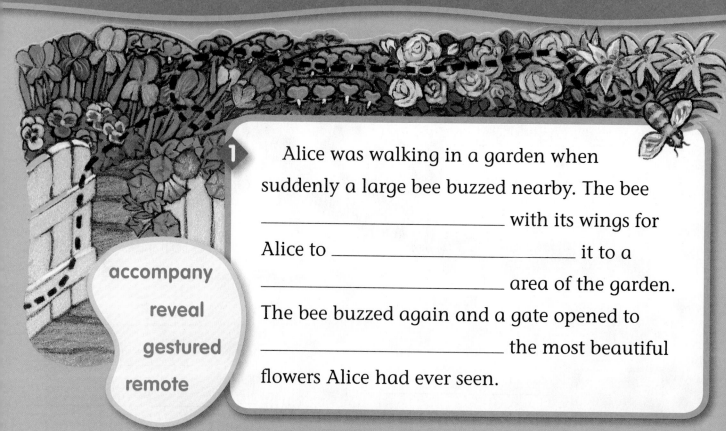

1

Alice was walking in a garden when suddenly a large bee buzzed nearby. The bee _____ with its wings for Alice to _____ it to a _____ area of the garden. The bee buzzed again and a gate opened to _____ the most beautiful flowers Alice had ever seen.

accompany

reveal

gestured

remote

2

Sara is an _____ girl who works hard at whatever she does. Last year she organized a project to _____ wildlife. Her community spirit helps her to _____ as a leader.

conserve

excel

industrious

Teacher: Read aloud the vocabulary words in the shapes. Then have students read the stories and write the best words to fill in the blanks. Ask students which words they chose to complete each story and why.

1 When might an **industrious** student finish his work?
- ○ after his classmates
- ○ before his classmates
- ○ same time as his classmates

2 Which would you be most likely to hear in a **remote** place?
- ○ birds singing
- ○ car horns honking
- ○ pet dogs yapping

3 When might you need to make a **gesture** instead of speak?
- ○ when you are tired
- ○ when your hand hurts
- ○ when your throat is sore

4 What would someone do if she wanted to **conserve** energy?
- ○ have every light in the house on
- ○ leave the refrigerator door open
- ○ turn off the heater when no one is home

5 What might you **reveal** to a best friend?
- ○ a secret
- ○ some pictures
- ○ your name

6 What would help you **excel** at sports?
- ○ a good friend
- ○ a new uniform
- ○ a healthy body

7 Where would you most likely **accompany** your teacher?
- ○ to the mall
- ○ to the library
- ○ on vacation

Teacher: Read aloud each numbered item and have students fill in the bubble next to the correct answer.

85

1 Laura's family was excited because Grandma was coming to visit. Mom was planning a special dinner. "I am going to make a **banquet**," she said.

banquet

2 Kirie moved to the United States from Japan. She is learning to speak English. Kirie gets lots of help from her **peers**.

peers

3 Each evening the campers share stories by the campfire. Everyone enjoys it when someone tells an **amusing** tale.

amusing

Teacher: Read aloud each numbered item. Have students write the vocabulary word under the picture that shows its meaning. Ask students which picture they chose and why.

Listen. Read. Write.

Outstanding

Arrival

Command

1

Josh in _____

Giving Ruff a bath was never easy. Ruff was splashing playfully in a tub of soapy water when he spotted a squirrel in the yard. He leapt from the tub, soapsuds flying everywhere. Josh yelled, "Sit, Ruff!" Ruff sat right down on the lawn.

2

_____

All of Dianna's drawings were good, but she wanted the picture for the art fair to be her best. She spent hours and hours on it. On the day of the fair, Dianna hurried over to her picture and she saw a blue ribbon. "Congratulations! Your picture wins first prize," said the judge.

3

Molly's _____

Joy had not seen her cousin Molly since she had moved to another state. Now Molly was coming to visit for a whole week! There was an announcement that Flight 202 was at the gate. Moments later Molly was running toward Joy. Together at last!

Teacher: Read aloud the vocabulary words at the top of the page. Have students read the stories and write a vocabulary word to complete each title. Ask students which words they chose to complete the titles and why.

87

Read. Listen. Write.

My dad is a terrific firefighter. Last week, Dad saved a family from a building that was on fire. Yesterday, the neighborhood had a special dinner to let him know how thankful they are.

We walked to the fire hall. I was so excited that I wanted to run. Dad just walked calmly, as if he were going to the corner store. When Dad walked into the hall, everyone cheered. After dinner other firefighters told stories about Dad. Some were serious stories about how he helps people, but others were very funny. At the end of the evening, everyone clapped for my dad. I had never felt so proud.

outstanding

amusing

strolled

banquet

peers

1. Dad is an _____ firefighter.

2. The neighborhood had a _____ for Dad.

3. Dad _____ to the fire hall.

4. Dad's _____ told stories about him.

5. Some of the stories were _____.

Teacher: Have students read the story. Then read the vocabulary words aloud. Have students read the sentences and write the vocabulary word that best completes each sentence. Ask students which words they wrote and why.

1 Which would you most likely find **amusing**?
- ○ an adventure story
- ○ a list of students' names
- ○ a recipe for making cocoa

2 Where would a boy find **peers**?
- ○ in his class
- ○ in an adult class
- ○ in a nursery

3 What might a person say upon her **arrival**?
- ○ "I am so sorry!"
- ○ "I hope to see you soon."
- ○ "Hello, how are you?"

4 How would a **stroll** most likely make you feel?
- ○ out of breath
- ○ peaceful
- ○ very sad

5 Who could give a **command**?
- ○ a tiny baby
- ○ a smart dog
- ○ a police officer

6 What might your teacher say if you turned in **outstanding** work?
- ○ "I am proud of you."
- ○ "Please try again."
- ○ "Where did you get this?"

7 Which might you have at a **banquet**?
- ○ a cheese sandwich
- ○ a decorated cake
- ○ cereal with fruit

Lesson 23

Listen. Read. Write.

dark
smooth
skate
twinkle
cloudy
dim
glow
sad
sparkle
slip
slide
shine

glide
glisten
gloomy

90

Teacher: Read aloud the vocabulary words that appear in each basket. Have students read the words on the vegetables and write each word under its related vocabulary word. Ask students which words they wrote on each basket and why.

Listen. Read. Write.

1 John ate an **entire** pie for dessert. "You ate a
_____ pie by yourself!"
his mother exclaimed.

whole
warm
apple

2 Anna **glided** very easily across the ice on her
skates. Her movements were very graceful and
_____.

bumpy
dangerous
smooth

3 **Traditions** are important to many people. These
practices help people _____
a special or important time.

remember
celebrate
forget

4 Gary is learning how to **steer** a car. He
practices every day, but he cannot seem to
_____ it yet.

control
wash
repair

5 Suzie's grandmother is full of **wisdom**. Suzie often
goes to her for _____ with
difficult problems.

money
dinner
help

Teacher: Read aloud each pair of sentences. Have students read the word choices and write
the best word to fill in the blank. Ask students which words they chose and why.

Listen. Read. Write.

1

The pond had finally frozen. The bright sun made the ice _____. Carrie put on her ice skates and _____ across the pond. To balance, she had to _____ her body carefully. Carrie could skate around the _____ pond without falling.

steer

glided

glisten

entire

2

Though cloudy skies made the day seem _____, nothing could spoil our family picnic. After an afternoon of enjoying hot dogs, watermelon, and baseball, it is a _____ to tell family stories. The older adults always end their stories with words of _____ for everyone.

gloomy

wisdom

tradition

92

1 Which would be more likely to **glisten**?
- ○ sunlight on ocean waves
- ○ lamplight on new carpet
- ○ moonlight over a desert

2 Which would be easiest to **glide** across?
- ○ a gravel parking lot
- ○ a frozen lake
- ○ a steep, rocky trail

3 Which would be hard for most people to **steer**?
- ○ a bicycle on a bike path
- ○ a car on a country road
- ○ a kite on a windy day

4 Which is an example of **gloomy** weather?
- ○ bright sunshine with no clouds
- ○ dark skies with heavy rains
- ○ brisk wind and cold temperatures

5 What might someone who ate an **entire** pizza say?
- ○ "I am so full."
- ○ "I am so bored."
- ○ "I am so excited."

6 Which of the following might be a **tradition**?
- ○ singing your favorite songs in the shower
- ○ brushing your teeth before bedtime
- ○ watching fireworks with your family

7 What would be a sign of **wisdom**?
- ○ saving your money for the future
- ○ buying only expensive things
- ○ losing your money while shopping

1 On hot days, Bill liked to fill his plastic swimming pool to the **brim**. The problem with this was that all of the water went over the _____ when he got in.

top

toys

yard

2 After shopping all day, Paul and his mother decided to have a **mellow** evening. They planned to _____ on the sofa and read a book.

relax

work

dance

3 The teacher told Hannah and Anna they had to **compromise** when they both wanted to read the same book. They _____ their problem by taking turns reading the book aloud.

solved

caused

liked

4 Amy's little brother was **persnickety** about his food. He was so _____ that he would eat nothing but canned peaches.

happy

lazy

picky

5 John is a good violinist because of his **perseverance**. He _____ gives up.

always

never

usually

Teacher: Read aloud each pair of sentences. Have students read the word choices and write the best word to fill in the blank. Ask students which words they chose and why.

Listen. Read. Write.

1

_____ Your Papers

Do you ever lose important papers? You can use a three-ringed binder to keep track of them. Divide the binder into sections and make a tab for each one. Sort your important papers and put them in the right parts of the notebook.

2

How to _____ Maggie

Maggie would rather play games with her friends all day than do her chores. One day, Dad came up with an idea. "Maggie, let's race to see how many dishes we can clear off the table in two minutes. Go!" Maggie got busy right away. Now Mom and Dad turn all of Maggie's chores into games.

3

_____ Pays Off

Eric started at a new school in November, but nobody paid much attention to him. Eric decided to be friendly to his classmates even if they ignored him. Soon, the other students started asking him to eat lunch with them. "Sometimes, a person just has to stay calm and not give up!" Eric thought.

Teacher: Read aloud the vocabulary words at the top of the page. Have students read the stories and write a vocabulary word to complete each title. Ask students which words they chose to complete the titles and why.

Jerry was nervous during his lunch with Uncle Max because Uncle Max complained about everything. First, his sandwich didn't have enough meat on it. Then his dessert was too sweet. Finally he was upset because the waiter filled his teacup up to the edge and tea spilled onto the tablecloth. "He needs to relax," thought Jerry. "Maybe I should just ask him to stop."

"I can't stop," said Uncle Max. "It is a habit."

"Hmm," thought Jerry. "What if every time you say something you don't like, you also say something you do like?" Uncle Max did not say anything until the waiter brought the bill. "I don't like having to pay this much for lunch," he said. Then he smiled at Jerry. "But I do like spending time with such a smart, nice boy."

persnickety

compromise

mellow

brim

motivated

1 At the beginning of the story, Jerry's Uncle Max was _____ about everything.

2 The teacup was full to the _____.

3 Jerry wanted Uncle Max to be _____.

4 Jerry suggested a _____ to help Uncle Max.

5 Jerry _____ Uncle Max to change.

Teacher: Have students read the story. Then read the vocabulary words aloud. Have students read the sentences and write the vocabulary word that best completes each sentence. Ask students which words they wrote and why.

1 What might **motivate** a person to get a job done?
- ○ a chance to do another chore
- ○ a chance to do something fun
- ○ a chance to pay some money

2 What might you say if you were **persnickety**?
- ○ "I only like soft, mushy food."
- ○ "I'll eat anything."
- ○ "What a tasty meal!"

3 What might a person who has **perseverance** say?
- ○ "Let me try again."
- ○ "I didn't really want to do this anyway."
- ○ "Who will do this for me?"

4 Which would you want your glass filled to the **brim** with?
- ○ a drink you don't like
- ○ a drink you do like
- ○ a drink that is a strange color

5 Whom might you **compromise** with?
- ○ a good friend
- ○ an ill-mannered bird
- ○ an unreasonable stranger

6 What is something you could **compile**?
- ○ a list of holidays
- ○ a pair of socks
- ○ a pot of soup

7 Which sound would make you feel **mellow**?
- ○ nails on a blackboard
- ○ screeching cats
- ○ singing birds

Teacher: Read aloud each numbered item and have students fill in the bubble next to the correct answer.

97

Words I Have Learned

 A

abrupt
abundant
accompany
achieve
adapt
admire
adorn
ambitious
amusing
anchor
anguish
anticipate
apology
appreciate
arrival
artistic
assemble
assist
assume
astonished
awe

 B

banquet
beaming
bizarre
blustery
boast
bout
brim

 C

carefree
ceremony
coincidence
comforting
command
companion
compile
compromise
conceal
confidence
confirm
consequence
conserve
contribute
creation

 D

dawdle
deceive
defeat
defiant
determined
diligent
diplomat
disappointed
disaster
discord
disguise
disgust
display
dreadful

 E

elegant
embarrass
emerald
emerge
entire
envy
excel
exhausted
expression

 F

fade
fasten
fleet
frisky

 G

gentle
gesture
giddy
glide
glimmer
glisten
gloomy
gracious
graze

 H

harsh
heave
hopeful
horizon
huddle
humane

I

idle
imaginative
indicate
individual
industrious
inscription
integrity

L

lonely

M

magnificent
majestic
mature
meadow
mellow
mischievous
motivate

N

nestle
nutritious

O

obvious
ominous
orbit
ordinary
organize
originality
outsmart
outstanding
ovation
overrun

P

paralyzed
patience
peers
perfect
performance
perseverance
persnickety
persuade
pesky
poised
pretend
priority
pursue

R

reluctant
remote
rescue
resemble
resourceful
restore
retreat
reveal

S

scan
scowl
scrawny
serious
shelter
slumber
smear
soothe
spectators
spiral
sprawl
squirm
stale
steer
stranded
strive

stroll
stylish
sympathy

T

talent
tease
thread
tilt
tradition
treacherous
tremble

V

variety
vendor
versatile
vibrant
victory
vital

W

warp
weary
wisdom

My Favorite Words

You can learn new words every day. Some of them you will always want to remember. So here is a place to write your favorite words!

_____   _____

_____   _____

_____   _____

_____   _____

_____   _____

_____   _____

_____   _____

_____   _____

_____   _____

_____   _____

_____   _____

_____   _____

Teacher: Invite students to tell favorite words they have learned. Ask them to explain why these words are favorites. Then have students write the words on this list. Encourage students to add to their lists as they learn to use new words, both in and out of the classroom.